About the ONCE UPON AMERICA® Series

Who is affected by the events of history? Not only the famous and powerful. Individuals from every part of society contribute a *story*—and so weave together *history*. Some of the finest storytellers bring their talents to this series of historical fiction, based on careful research and designed specifically for readers ages 7–11. These are tales of young people growing up in a young, dynamic country. Each ONCE UPON AMERICA® volume shapes readers' understanding of the people who built America and of their own roles in our unfolding history. For history is a story that we continue to write, with a chapter for each of us beginning "Once upon America."

D0058506

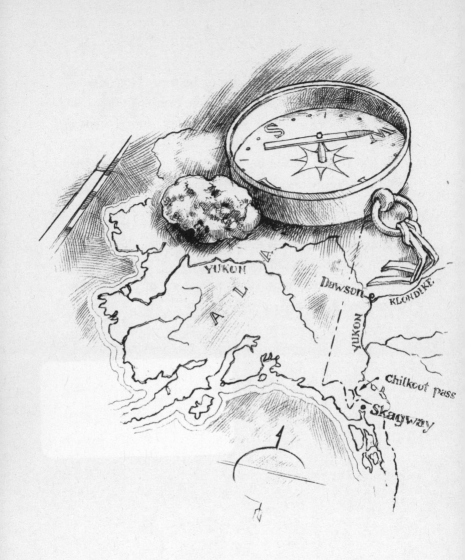

The Bite of the Gold Bug

A STORY OF THE ALASKAN GOLD RUSH

BY BARTHE DeCLEMENTS

ILLUSTRATED BY DAN ANDREASEN

PUFFIN BOOKS

I wish to express my thanks to Eric Kimmel, who sent me the magnificent book of photographs, The Klondike Quest; my thanks to the members of Seanache who critiqued the chapters of the manuscript and lent me their books on the Alaskan gold rush; my thanks to my nephew, Ralph DeClements, who sent me his book on Alaska; and my thanks to my son, Christopher Greimes, and my daughter, Mari DeClements, for their invaluable input on the structure of this story.

PUFFIN BOOKS
Published by the Penguin Group
Penguin Books USA Inc., 375 Hudson Street, New York, New York 10014, U.S.A.
Penguin Books Ltd, 27 Wrights Lane, London W8 5TZ, England
Penguin Books Australia Ltd, Ringwood, Victoria, Australia
Penguin Books Canada Ltd, 10 Alcorn Avenue, Toronto, Ontario, Canada M4V 3B2
Penguin Books (N.Z.) Ltd, 182-190 Wairau Road, Auckland 10, New Zealand

Penguin Books Ltd, Registered Offices: Harmondsworth, Middlesex, England

First published in the United States of America by Viking,
a division of Penguin Books USA Inc., 1992
Published in Puffin Books, 1994

19 20 21 22

Text copyright © Barthe DeClements, 1992
Illustrations copyright © Dan Andreasen, 1992
All rights reserved

ONCE UPON AMERICA® is a registered trademark of Viking Penguin,
a division of Penguin Books USA Inc.

THE LIBRARY OF CONGRESS HAS CATALOGED THE VIKING EDITION AS FOLLOWS:

DeClements, Barthe.
The bite of the gold bug / by Barthe DeClements;
illustrated by Dan Andreasen.   p.   cm.—(Once upon America)
Summary: Bucky and his father, prospecting for gold in Alaska in 1898,
must overcome storms, dangerous mountain trails, and wilderness
predators before confronting the final challenge of human treachery.
ISBN 0-670-84495-0
[1. Gold mines and mining—Fiction. 2. Alaska—Fiction.]
I. Andreasen, Dan, ill. II. Title. III. Series.
PZ7.D3584Bi   1992   [Fic]—dc20   91-39363   CIP   AC

Puffin Books ISBN 0-14-036081-6

Printed in the United States of America
Set in Goudy Oldstyle

Except in the United States of America, this book is sold subject to the condition that
it shall not, by way of trade or otherwise, be lent, re-sold, hired out, or otherwise
circulated without the publisher's prior consent in any form of binding or cover
other than that in which it is published and without a similar condition
including this condition being imposed on the subsequent purchaser.

*This book is dedicated to the memory of my father,
Ralph DeClements, an adventurous man.*

Contents

The Mosquitoes Are as Big as Hummingbirds   1

Itchy Wool Drawers   8

The Old Man and the Little Dog   16

The Golden Stairs   22

Overboard   29

Gold   36

Uncle Tanner Weakens   44

About This Book   55

The Mosquitoes Are as Big as Hummingbirds

I nibbled at the piece of apple dumpling on my spoon. My sister, Nellie, stood across the table from me with her hands on her hips, a look of impatience on her face.

Ma said, "Nellie, you don't have to wait for Bucky. You've cleared enough of the table. Go into the sitting room and read your book."

After Nellie left, Ma said to me, "Hurry up with your dessert, Bucky. Uncle Tanner and Pa and I want to talk."

I knew they did. That's why I was eating slowly.

The last time Uncle Tanner had visited, he'd brought presents for all of us. This time he was trying to talk Ma out of her and Pa's savings.

Ma was careful with money. "If we all try," she said, "we can put away enough money so Pa can have his own hardware store someday."

Pa worked six days a week in Mr. Hadden's store. But it wasn't easy to save because Mr. Hadden paid his clerks poorly. We didn't have much, and Pa wanted more for us.

That was the point Uncle Tanner was trying to make to Ma. So far, I didn't think he was succeeding.

"What I don't understand, Tanner," she told him, "is where all that gold went that you brought down from Alaska."

"Well, let's just say the winning cards weren't dealt my way."

"You mean you lost thousands of dollars gambling?" Ma's voice was sharp now.

"Now, Hope, Tanner dug up the gold. He could do what he pleased with it." Pa's words were meant to calm Ma. As I quietly spooned up another tiny bite of apple dumpling, I guessed that Pa already had decided to go to Alaska with Ma's brother.

"I just got in with some sharpshooters, Hope." Uncle Tanner pulled on his handlebar mustache as he hurried to explain. "That won't happen again. If you

and Clint will pay for this trip to the Yukon, I'll get back all the gold I lost and more. And after I transfer half my claim to Clint, he'll come home a rich man."

"We've done all right so far," Ma snapped. "It's our savings you're asking for. And you already have one partner, so Clint would only get one-half of your share."

"Emmett and I staked the claim in the fall of 1896. When I came down here in the fall of '97, I had $3,000. I bet half of that is more than Clint can save in seven years."

"Tanner has a point, Hope," Pa put in. "It will take us seven more years to save enough to buy my own store. By that time, Bucky and Nellie will be grown-up."

He was right! In four days, I'd be twelve. In seven years, I'd be almost *nineteen.*

"How much does it cost to get outfitted for this trip?" Ma sounded nicer now, but still cautious.

"The North West Mounted Police check everyone's supplies at Chilkoot Pass. Each man has to have a year's worth of food or he'll be turned back."

"And how much do the supplies cost?" Ma insisted.

"Well, they usually cost about $500 for each person. It won't cost that much for us because Emmett and I already have the mining equipment. But it's smart to have a little extra to hire a wagon to get through

Skagway, Alaska. Soapy Smith rules that place and he and his gang rob anyone they can catch."

"How do you go the rest of the way?" Ma asked. "It must be a thousand miles to Dawson City."

A thousand miles! I tried to imagine how far that was. Ma looked down the table at me. I quickly dipped my spoon back into my bowl. I didn't want to be excused from the table.

"We hike to Lake Bennett," Uncle Tanner answered Ma. "From there, I can get us a free ride on the Yukon River to Dawson because I know how to pilot through the rapids."

Ma turned to Pa. "It sounds like this trip will take months and use up most of our savings. How will the children and I live while you're gone, Clint?"

I guess Pa didn't have an answer for that, but Uncle Tanner did. "You've got four bedrooms. Put Nellie in with you and rent out two of your rooms. The hotels can't hold the families the stampeders bring in."

I knew *stampeders* was the name given to the people who jammed into town from all over the country. They'd been coming ever since last summer when *The Seattle Post-Intelligencer* ran a big headline: GOLD! GOLD! GOLD! GOLD!

"I don't think two roomers would feed us and pay our bills," Ma said.

"You'd have plenty of money if you rented three

rooms. It wouldn't cost us much to add a boy," Uncle Tanner said. "We could take—"

Ma quickly interrupted him. "Bucky, go in the sitting room with Nellie."

I slowly put down my spoon.

"You git!" Pa ordered.

Ma didn't come into the sitting room until nine-thirty. And then it was just to kiss Nellie and me goodnight and tell us to go right to bed. As Nellie and I climbed the stairs Ma went back to the dining room.

It seemed as if I'd barely fallen asleep when I felt someone sit on my bed. It was Pa. "Would you like to travel to Alaska with me and your uncle?" he asked.

"You bet!" I said.

"I have to warn you, Bucky. This trip is going to be rugged."

"That's all right," I told him. "I can make it."

Pa gave me a pat on my shoulder. "Then get up. We have to go to the outfitter's."

Uncle Tanner was telling Nellie stories about the Yukon Territory when I got to the breakfast table. "Everything up there is huge. Even the mosquitoes are as big as hummingbirds. I saw a grizzly bear up there whose neck was bigger than my waist."

Ma passed me a bowl of hot oatmeal. Her eyes were opened as wide as Nellie's.

Pa wiped his mouth on his napkin and stood up.

"Don't you think we should get the list of supplies made out, Tanner?"

I thought so, too. If my uncle kept on talking, Ma would change her mind about letting me go to Alaska.

Itchy Wool Drawers

While Nellie cleared the breakfast table, Ma sat with me. She was looking awfully sad. "Bucky, when you go with your pa to get supplies, I want you to buy something for yourself." She took a fifty-cent piece out of her apron pocket and put it in my hand.

I tried to give it back. "Ma, you'll need the money."

"No, I was going to spend it on a birthday present for you." Tears puddled in her eyes and she grabbed me and kissed me.

I took the fifty cents with me to the outfitter's. Pa and Uncle Tanner had a long list of supplies. Split peas—400 pounds, bacon—400 pounds, flour—900 pounds, beans—300 pounds, salt—25 pounds, rolled oats—90 pounds, condensed milk—4 dozen cans, evaporated potatoes—60 pounds, evaporated apples, peaches, and pears, tobacco, soap, matches . . .

While they gathered supplies, I wandered around the store trying to decide what to buy with my four bits. I probably wouldn't have spotted the mosquito netting if it hadn't been tied with red ribbon. I gave the clerk my fifty-cent piece, and he gave me a dime in return.

When I joined Uncle Tanner and Pa in the clothing section, Uncle Tanner asked me how much the netting weighed.

I read the tag. "Fourteen ounces."

"That's almost a pound. We'll be lugging our loads up mountains. You don't want to put any extra weight in your pack."

"That's all right. I'll carry it."

Uncle Tanner shook his head, and Pa looked thoughtful. I kept a grip on my package. The grizzly bears didn't worry me much, but the big mosquitoes did.

"Here," Pa said, holding a pair of gray wool drawers up to my waist. "Do you think these will fit you?"

"They're a little long," I said. They looked itchy, too.

"That's as small as they come." Uncle Tanner was pawing through the piles of underclothes. He glanced back at me. "You have to have some room to grow. You can stuff the ends in your boots. Try this undershirt."

Boots! I didn't know I was going to get boots. I agreed to the undershirt fast so we could get over to the boots. Pa got leather ones and rubber ones, and so did I.

Mine were too big for me. I ignored that and clumped into our house to show them off to Ma and Nellie. Ma smiled, but Nellie just shrugged and said, "At least your feet won't get eaten by mosquitoes."

"And neither will my face. Look what I got for my birthday present." I pulled my mosquito netting from the package, untied the ribbon, and flapped out the eight yards.

Nellie wasn't impressed. Her attention was on the red ribbon. "That's not for a boy. That's for a girl's hair."

"No," I said, "it's for my netting."

The ship to Alaska was leaving at ten o'clock in the morning. By the time I got down to breakfast, everyone was rushing around the house, getting ready to leave for the docks. Uncle Tanner's fur hat was tilted to one side of his head and his black eyes were snapping with impatience.

"Hurry up and eat, Bucky," he said to me. "There will be 200 men fighting for places on the boat."

Nellie and Ma came down to the waterfront to see us off. The place was crawling with people lugging their baggage. Pa lifted a sack of flour onto his shoulder. "Here, take the boots."

I picked up the string of spare boots and followed Pa onto a steamship. The deck was so crowded with passengers that we had to elbow our way to the ladder leading to the hold.

We could hardly wiggle our way past the crates and pens and boxes to stow our gear under the bunks. At least bunks was what one of the crew called them when he pointed out ours. They were just rough wooden boards nailed to the inside of the ship.

I heard a bleating behind me and turned to peek into one of the pens. "Pa!" I said. "We aren't going to sleep down here with goats, are we?"

Pa raised one eyebrow. "I guess we are."

Uncle Tanner made his way through the hold, carrying a load on each shoulder. Just as we finished stowing the last sack of cornmeal there was a blast from the ship's whistle. We pushed through the crowd and out to the dock, where Ma and Nellie were waiting.

Ma handed me the sack she'd been carrying. "Tomorrow's March tenth, your birthday. I got up this morning and made you a cake."

"Coconut! Thanks. That's my favorite."

"I know," she said.

After Pa kissed Ma, he lifted up Nellie to give her the last hug. She locked her arms around his neck and cried into his chest. She was only nine, after all.

The boat's whistle blasted again, and Uncle Tanner tugged on Pa's jacket. "We have to go."

I dug into my pocket, took out the dime I had left, and gave it to Nellie. "Here, buy your doll some new shoes."

Her face was pink and wet, but she gave me a little smile and wave.

With all the miners and gear aboard, I was afraid we'd sink when we pulled away from the dock. Pa checked the side of the ship. "She's riding pretty low in the water," he told Uncle Tanner.

We kept afloat, though. I climbed on top of a lifeboat and played my harmonica all the way through Puget Sound. The sky darkened after we passed Vancouver Island, and the ship ran into a storm. Waves dashed over the bow and soaked the deck.

I stayed in my bunk for two days. I wasn't the only seasick passenger. The hold stank of vomit and goats. I tried to get relief by sleeping, but a little dog

inside a crate whimpered the whole night long.

On the third day, the ship stopped rolling, my belly settled, and I climbed shakily up the ladder to let the salty wind revive me. After supper that night, Pa, Uncle Tanner and I ate the coconut birthday cake. Even three days old, it was delicious.

On the fifth day, Uncle Tanner leaned over the boat railing and said to me, "There she is."

"Where? Where?" I squinted at the distant land. All I could see were shacks, tents, and piles of logs lining the shore.

He pointed in the direction of the shacks.

"That's Skagway, Alaska?" I couldn't believe it. "Where's the dock?"

"There is no dock. See those barges coming toward our ship? They're going to unload us."

"But . . . but those barges are too big to go near the shore. How does everyone get their stuff to dry land?"

"The stampeders are going to carry theirs." He gave me a friendly slap on my back. "But *we're* taking ours on a wagon."

The Old Man
and the
Little Dog

By the time we'd loaded the wagon, the water came halfway over the wheels and up to the bellies of the horses. Sweat broke out on my forehead as the wagon teetered through the tide flats. Every second, I figured we and all our supplies were going over the side.

I didn't feel sorry for the men who were wading in the water with their gear on their backs. At least they were sure their flour would be dry when they reached the shore.

When the wagon wheels finally rolled onto gravel, I said, "I'm glad that's over."

"That's nothing to what's ahead," Uncle Tanner replied.

The wagoner drove us through the town of Skagway. The main road was even muddier than the tide flats had been. There were shacky stores on either side of the mud. One sign on the front of a store said, JEFF. SMITHS PARLOR.

"Is that Soapy Smith's place?" I asked.

"That's it," Uncle Tanner answered grimly. "But he won't be in. He'll be out on the shore pretending to help people with their baggage while he robs them of everything they own."

We went past rows of tents, and on up through the trees, and on toward Dyea. We rode until the Dyea River entered a canyon and the trail narrowed to a footpath. The driver yanked the horses to a halt and helped us unload the wagon.

After he left, Pa, my uncle, and I strapped packs to our shoulders. Before we began our hike, I looked down at the rest of our boxes on the ground. "Won't someone steal them?"

"Not up here," Uncle Tanner said. "Any man caught carrying goods marked with someone else's name is tied to a post and whipped. Come on. Let's move ahead."

What was ahead were fallen logs, twisted roots, and slippery boulders. The icy path crossed and recrossed the freezing river. We climbed higher and higher and the air got colder and colder until my fingers stiffened in my mittens. Whenever we hit flat ground, we dumped our packs and trudged back for another load.

We did this over and over, until we'd covered the trail twenty times. Once when I collapsed on a rock because my knees gave out, Uncle Tanner checked my pack. "What are these?" he said, pulling out my schoolbooks.

"Ma gave me those. She didn't want me to get behind in my grammar."

Uncle Tanner tossed them to the side of the trail. I was so tired, I didn't care.

The days and nights of the endless trek blurred in my mind until one afternoon we passed a young man and woman. Staggering behind them was an old man. He carried the little dog that had whined beneath me in the ship's hold.

Uncle Tanner shook his head over the group. I knew he thought they were stupid to try this trip. I thought I was a little stupid, too.

Uncle Tanner spurted ahead when we neared a second hollow in the mountains. "We're at the Scales!" he shouted.

This was the last resting and weighing-in place before we climbed to Chilkoot Pass. I hurried to catch up with my uncle. "See the Golden Stairs?" He pointed up the mountain.

My heart sank to my boots. Straight up a sheer white

incline marched a single line of stampeders. They looked like a row of black ants crawling toward the heavens. "We're going up there?" My legs would never make it.

"Dump your pack here," Uncle Tanner told my pa. Pa dumped it and left me sitting on the bacon box while they went back for another load.

I was flapping my arms, trying to keep warm, when the man and woman we had passed on the trail put down their load beside ours. The old man was with them and he squatted on a flour sack after they left. The little dog shivered on his lap.

"What's he got on his feet?" I asked the old man.

He held up one of the dog's paws. "Moccasins. I made her leather moccasins."

I told the old man that my name was Bucky. He told me his was Mr. Martin. He was traveling with his daughter and son-in-law.

Mr. Martin said his son-in-law had been bitten by the gold bug. "He thinks he's going to pan a million dollars out of the Klondike River."

"My uncle says the gold isn't in the Klondike. It's in the creeks around the river," I told Mr. Martin. "And my uncle says all the good claims were staked out a year and a half ago, in the fall of '96."

"That so?" Mr. Martin had cut a hunk of blanket off his bedroll and was tying it around his dog's middle with a piece of rope.

He sat the dog up on its hind legs and asked, "Is that better, Trixie?"

It didn't seem much better. The dog was still shivering.

When Pa and Uncle Tanner came back, Uncle Tanner put up our tent. Pa built a fire with the wood they carried with them. I melted snow over the fire and soaked dried apples in the water.

The apples tasted pretty good when I stirred them into my beans, but at night I dreamed of Ma's coconut cake.

The Golden Stairs

It took another day and a half for Pa and Uncle Tanner to bring in the rest of our supplies. Pa had them weighed on the scales. Then he spent the afternoon bargaining with Indian packers. Some of them wanted to charge a dollar a pound to carry supplies over the pass. Pa made a deal with two Indians for 70 cents a pound. They agreed to start the next morning.

I woke up to the smell of coffee and crawled out of the tent. Uncle Tanner was talking to Pa as he shoveled flapjacks from the frying pan onto aluminum plates. "You can't stop on the climb. If you get out of line, you might not get in again for three hours."

"How long does it take to get up to the pass?" I asked.

"About six hours," Uncle Tanner said.

While I chewed on my stack of flapjacks, I wondered what happened if you had to pee. I didn't want to seem like a baby and ask that, but I did ask, "How long does it take to get back down the mountain?"

Uncle Tanner grinned. "About six minutes."

Before I could find out why, the two Indians arrived. They waited silently by themselves until Pa finished his coffee.

Uncle Tanner loaded the Indians first. They were used to the climb and could carry 100 pounds each. He loaded 70 pounds on Pa's back, along with one of the shovels, and 70 on his, along with another shovel. Then he asked me to get him my mosquito netting.

"What for?" I didn't want to give it up. "There aren't any mosquitoes here."

"Just hurry and get it." When Uncle Tanner's ready to go, he's ready to go.

I pulled the netting slowly out of my pack. He snatched it from me, undid the ribbon, stuffed the red ribbon in his jacket pocket, and tossed me back the loose netting. I carried it with me while we hiked to the Golden Stairs.

I watched the Indians grasp the rope behind Pa. The

fur on their hoods spiked up around their dark faces. Uncle Tanner got in line behind the Indians. The big crate on his back almost bent him double. He held on to the rope with one hand and poked a stick into the snow with the other. Both he and Pa wore dark-colored glass spectacles so the sun reflecting off the snow wouldn't burn their eyes.

I must have watched them climb for two hours. They inched along with their heavy loads, sometimes slipping onto their stomachs. When they blurred into the black line of climbers, I went back and sat on our bacon box. Mr. Martin and Trixie were there.

"How do you think they get down from the pass in six minutes, if it takes them six hours to climb up?" I asked Mr. Martin.

"Look." He pointed up the mountain. A dark blob whizzed over the snow and around the boulders. I stared until it came closer. A man was sledding down the mountain on a shovel.

When Pa and Uncle Tanner came sailing down late in the afternoon, I told Pa it looked like fun. He shook his head and took off his glasses. His eyes were rimmed with red. So were Uncle Tanner's. I made the fire while they rested in our tent.

The next morning, I asked them to take me with them on the day's trip to the summit. "Let him come," my uncle said to Pa. "It'll be easier to take him now. We're liable to be worn out in a week."

In a week! By my figuring, it was already April. "When do we get to Dawson City?"

Uncle Tanner thought a minute. "We need to be at Lake Bennett when the ice breaks up at the end of May. That way we'll be on one of the first boats going down the river rapids. We should reach Dawson in June."

I was quiet while I helped take down the tent and fold it into Uncle Tanner's pack. I'd thought we must be near the end of our trip. Instead, we were only halfway.

When we got to the summit trail, Uncle Tanner warned me as he'd warned Pa. "Everyone on the rope takes a step at the same time. It's called the Chilkoot lockstep. You can't hold up the line."

He let the Indians go first. He went next, then Pa, then me. "If your hand slips off the rope, grab onto my leg, Bucky," Pa said.

"I'll be fine," I said. And I was—for the first few hours. Uncle Tanner had told me there were 1,500 steps cut into the icy mountain, and I was counting them, one by one.

About noon, the April sun began to melt the ice. My feet slid around in my large leather boots and my boots slid around on the ice.

"Git!" the man behind me said.

I tried. I had both hands on the rope, pulling myself forward. I'd lost my pole on step 523.

"Mush on, boy. Mush on!" the man behind me muttered.

The trail was so steep everyone's face was three feet from the ground. When the man said "Mush on" again, I took a quick step, my boot slipped, and I crashed backwards onto the man's head.

Pa turned around to grab me and missed. The man told Pa, "This boy's petered out. He ain't going to make it."

I scrambled up the steps on my hands and knees until Pa could help me stand. A grumble of anger came from the men stalled below us. Pa loosened the straps holding the crate on his shoulders and let it slide onto the snow beside the trail.

He took my pack and handed it to Uncle Tanner, who had stopped ahead of us. The angry grumble became louder. "Get off the trail! Get off the trail!" the men below us hollered.

"Bucky, climb on my back—fast." Pa bent down and I jumped on his back. He and Uncle Tanner faced up the mountain and started the lockstep again. The grumbling faded.

The sun beat on me. Sweat poured off my forehead and into my eyes. I couldn't let go of Pa to wipe it away. My wool underwear itched, but I couldn't scratch. The colored spectacles that were too big for me had fallen off my face when I'd crashed into the

man. I tried to keep my burning eyes closed. I knew sun on snow could blind me.

Pa climbed higher and higher and higher. The sharp edge of his shovel cut into my side as he heaved himself up, step after step. The clouds covered the sun and a freezing wind blew. I shivered and felt Pa shiver under me. Then I felt his right leg give.

"Get down," he ordered.

I slid from his back. He twisted around, grabbed me by my waist, and set me up in front of him. "March," he said. "Quick!"

I marched, quick, before the muttering behind us could swell. I marched and marched. Each time my feet slipped in my boots and my boots slipped on the ice, I went down on my hands and knees. Each time I went down, Pa pulled me up.

My wet gloves froze and my fingers went numb. Snow swirled in with the wind, covering my eyelashes until I could barely see. I hurt so bad, I cried to myself and the tears stung my face.

Still we marched on and on and on. The groans of the men pounded a dull rhythm in my head as I lifted one frozen boot after the other. On and on and on.

Overboard

"We're here, son." Pa's voice floated around me, and I felt rough woolen blankets against my face. "Drink this."

I drank. "Hot chocolate," I whispered through swollen lips. "It's good."

"And you're good, too." Pa was sitting on the tent floor beside me. "You made it to the Chilkoot Pass."

I stayed in the tent most of the days it took Pa and Uncle Tanner to bring up the rest of our gear. When I did poke my head out of the door flap and into the howling wind, I saw my red ribbon flying from a pole. The pole was stuck in a snow-covered mound to mark our pile of supplies. There must have been thousands of white mounds spread over the ground.

We didn't need the marker after we made the long hike down the other side of the pass and on to Lake Bennett. There were a thousand more crates and sacks sitting in front of tents, but the snow had melted in the May sun. We waited for the ice to melt on the lake.

"I thought the lake would have sand around it instead of chunks of rock," I told Pa, who was sitting on a log with me.

"Listen," Pa said. "I think I hear the ice creak."

"I can't hear anything," I complained. "Just pounding and sawing. I can't even sleep because all the men work on their boats until the sun goes down. And it goes down later and later every night."

"I don't think it goes down at all in the summer," Pa said. "And everyone wants to sail to Dawson instead of walking 500 more miles. Don't you?"

"I guess so." I was feeling crabby.

We watched Uncle Tanner walk around the curve of the lake toward us. He was smiling as he plopped himself next to Pa. "I got us our free ride, Clint. It took me all morning to find a watertight craft. Not ten percent of those stampeders have even built a raft before."

That evening, while I was eating my beans, a low rumble came from the lake. "There she goes," Pa said.

He was right. By the next morning, huge chunks of ice were bobbing across the lake.

"Where's all that ice going?" I asked.

Uncle Tanner laughed. "The same place we're going. Down the Yukon River."

It was about the first of June when we got on the boat. The last patches of snow had barely melted before the mosquitoes came out. They weren't as big as hummingbirds, but they flew in huge swarms. Each time I slapped my forehead, I hit fifteen of them.

Two Norwegians had built the boat. They couldn't talk English very well. They mostly smiled and nodded their heads. Their boat was wide, with railings on the sides. There was a mast in the middle and a long tiller in back.

We sailed across the lake and down the Yukon. Whenever the wind died, Pa and the Norwegians poled the boat around the rocks. Uncle Tanner stayed in back and worked the tiller. I leaned over the railing and watched the shore.

When I spotted two bears walking along the beach, I went crazy. "Pa! Pa!" I yelled. "See over there! They're grizzlies. They've got humps!"

The big one turned to look at us. Her mouth was hanging open and it was wide enough to stick your head in.

"I'd sure like to have that little one," I said.

"You touch that little one," my uncle said, "and that mama bear will swat you over the mountain."

The river narrowed and the tree-lined shore changed to rock walls a hundred feet high. Uncle Tanner nodded to Pa. "This is it."

"Sit in the middle, Bucky," Pa told me. "Be quiet and hold on."

Another boat came up close behind us. Before I thought, I blurted out, "There's Mr. Martin and Trixie!"

"Be quiet," Pa ordered.

It was then I noticed the water beside our boat was swirling rapidly under the bow. I twisted my head to follow the water. It circled into the middle of the river and sank into a giant whirlpool, not ten feet in front of us.

I snapped my head back to see Uncle Tanner clutching the tiller and shouting, "Shore! Shore! Get closer to the shore."

Pa and the Norwegians rammed their poles into the water. Inch by inch, they pushed us toward the wall of rocks. I held my breath as we slid beside the whirlpool.

The swirling water sucked the boat from one side. The rocks banged it on the other. Pa and the Norwegians pounded the floor of the river with their poles. Uncle Tanner held on to the tiller with all his weight.

Water poured over the side of the boat as we spun around the edge of the whirlpool. And then, suddenly, the boat righted and we were floating in flat water. "Boy, that was scary," I said.

All the men laughed, but the Norwegians' white faces made me think they'd been scared, too. I rose up from my seat, looking for Mr. Martin. "Get back down," Pa ordered.

"But I want to see if Mr. Martin's boat is safe."

Pa glanced behind us. "They're all right. They're coming. They must have followed us."

Mr. Martin was no dummy, I thought to myself. I leaned over to get a cracker out of our food sack.

"Stay down, Bucky," Uncle Tanner said.

I stared up at him, bewildered. I *was* down.

"We've still got the rapids to get through," Pa explained.

Rapids? I'd forgotten about the rapids. I switched around on my seat to watch for them. About a mile down the river, the water turned frothy. A few seconds later, it was boiling and we were flying.

With Uncle Tanner working the tiller, we zipped around boulders at lightning speed. We flew down banks of white water and swerved away from gravel bars. The big, flat boat nosed up into the air, slapped back onto the river, and rose again.

"Yoweee!" I yelled.

The water simmered for a stretch, the boat rocked,

the water boiled, and we were off once more.

When the last of the bubbles disappeared and the river turned green, my heartbeats slowed with the boat. The Norwegians each rose and shook Uncle Tanner's hand.

Pa was looking up the river behind us. "Is Mr. Martin coming?" I asked him.

"Nope, they didn't make it, Bucky."

I jumped to my feet. "We have to go back and save them!"

"They'll get to shore," Pa said, pointing up the beach. "Your friends aren't the only ones who've cracked up."

There on the beach were broken crates, a mangled raft, an overturned boat, and two men pulling wet sacks out of the water.

"Poor Mr. Martin." I sat down in our boat with a bump.

All the way to Dawson I kept thinking of the little dog, Trixie, and her little moccasins.

"Don't worry," Pa told me. "Dogs can swim."

I sure hoped Trixie could.

Gold

I was asleep on the bottom of the boat when we arrived at Dawson City late one afternoon. "Will you look at that," I heard Uncle Tanner say. "They've built a post office!"

"Where?" I sat up, batting mosquitoes away from my face.

"Right in the middle of town." There was such pride in his voice that I expected to see a brick building.

Instead it was just a log one. A line of men stood in front of its door. Pa hopped out of the boat and onto the muddy ground. "Maybe there's a letter from Seattle."

While Pa got in the line, Uncle Tanner and I plowed through the mud up to the boardwalk. We walked along Front Street, gawking at the signs that hung on the tents.

"This is like a carnival," I said. It was.

People were selling everything: stoves, gold scales, axes, waffles and coffee, long johns, fresh bread, haircuts. I came to a halt at the lemonade stand. The sign said, ICE COLD LEMONADE 25¢. A woman in a long skirt waited by the table under the canvas awning.

I looked up at Uncle Tanner. Twenty-five cents was a lot of money for a cup of lemonade. Things were a lot cheaper in Seattle.

"We-ell," he said. "I guess I can spare four bits."

Pa came up to us while we were standing on the boardwalk, drinking our lemonade. He was smiling over an envelope he was carrying. "You got a letter from Ma?" I asked. "How could her letter get here before we did?"

"On boats that travel around the Alaskan coast and up the Yukon," Uncle Tanner told me.

I stared at my uncle and then at Pa. "You mean we could have come all this way on a boat?"

"If we'd had that much money, we could have." Pa handed me the letter and took my cup to drink the last of the lemonade. I pretended I didn't mind, but

I would have liked five cups all to myself.

Ma wrote that she had rented our three bedrooms to wives of Alaskan miners. She was making strawberry jam and Nellie was swimming in Green Lake and they missed us. There was a note from Nellie scrawled on the bottom of the last page: "Have you seen any bears yet?"

I would write her about the baby bear, I thought. Homesickness flooded over me. I kept my head bowed while Uncle Tanner and Pa discussed hiring a horse and wagon to haul our stuff to the gold claim.

They hired two of the skinniest horses I'd ever seen. There wasn't much grass to eat, I guess. The poor horses had to pull us and all our supplies through two feet of mud down Dawson's Front Street.

"How much farther is it to your cabin?" I kept asking Uncle Tanner as we traveled along the Klondike River.

"It's up this trail," he finally said.

While we rode on the mountain trail, I kept expecting it to end on the bank of a pretty flowing stream. It ended in piles of mud and gravel.

Running along the side of the piles was a winding wooden trough. "What's that for?" I asked.

"That's a sluice box," Uncle Tanner said. "Come on. I'll show you how it works. See the wooden ribs spaced along the bottom of the box?"

I nodded as I bent over the trough.

"You shovel the pay dirt into the top of the box,

run water from the creek over the dirt, and the gold in the muck gets caught in the ribs we call riffles."

I frowned up at my uncle. "Why doesn't some of the muck get caught, too?"

"Some of it does. But gold is heavy and it falls to the bottom. You have to clean out the riffles and pan out the gold. I'll show you tomorrow. Let's go help your pa."

We helped Pa carry our gear to the cabin, which was hidden behind a mine shaft. A man with a scraggly gray beard was sitting on the steps smoking a pipe. "Thought you'd come today," he said. "I caught you a mess of fish for dinner."

Uncle Tanner dumped his load on the ground and he and the man pounded each other on the back. "This is Emmett," my uncle said. "And this is Clint and Bucky."

Emmett's pants were held together with a pin. He seemed dirty to me. Then I looked at Pa and saw that we were raggedy and dirty, too.

"Come in. Come in." Emmett popped up the cabin steps and held the door open for us.

The inside of the little log cabin surprised me. The floor was swept clean. On one wall were shelves and hooks holding frying pans, cups, books, jackets and suspenders. Another wall had four bunks with black bearskins on them. One bottom bunk held a bedroll. I guessed it belonged to Emmett.

We put our supplies on the shelves of the third wall. Against the fourth wall was a fat iron stove. In front of that stood a table and benches made of logs sawed in half.

"This is nice," I said, going over to stroke the bearskin on a top bunk. "Did you shoot the bears?"

"Yep, I did," Emmett said. "Black bears make warm mattresses."

"Not grizzlies?"

He shook his shaggy gray head. "I'm not taking on no grizzlies."

In my next load from the wagon, I carried my bedroll and my mosquito netting. "Do you have a hammer and nails?" I asked Emmett.

He got them for me and I nailed the mosquito netting to the wall and posts of a top bunk. I'd given Emmett back his hammer and was winding up the red ribbon when Pa came in with his load. "That's a smart boy you've got there," Emmett told him.

After we'd finished the fish dinner and I'd crawled into my bed, I felt smart, too. I could hear Pa and Uncle Tanner slap and curse the mosquitoes singing in the night. Giggling to myself, I went peacefully off to sleep.

"How come you put up four bunks?" I said to Emmett while we were eating our sourdough flapjacks the next morning.

"Your uncle wrote me you were coming."

I asked to be passed the maple syrup. Emmett handed it to me before he said to Uncle Tanner, "I didn't see any syrup in the new supplies."

"We lost a crate on the Chilkoot," Pa told him.

I waited for Emmett to ask why, but he didn't. I put down the can of syrup and ate the rest of my flapjacks dry.

"You were here alone last winter, Emmett," Pa said.

"Yep," he agreed. "Every morning I built a bonfire on the frozen ground, and when the fire went out I dug out the thawed muck and gravel. You saw those dumps out there? Lucky I hit a pay streak before my fingers froze."

Uncle Tanner leaned forward. "You think you hit a pay streak?"

"Yep, I washed some of it down and there's colors all right."

Uncle Tanner concentrated on gobbling his breakfast, fast. He didn't even stop to wipe off his mustache between gulps of coffee.

"What happened to your fingers?" I asked Emmett.

"Frostbite. Had to spend three days soaking them in kerosene. Saved them, though. Gets 50 degrees below zero here. You have to watch your fingers and your nose. If you've got a partner, he can warn you if a piece of your face turns white."

Uncle Tanner pushed himself away from the table.

"Let's get that sluice box going."

I followed them outdoors. Emmett scooped some dirt out of the riffles and into a gold pan before he turned the water into the sluice box. While Pa and Uncle Tanner shoveled muck and gravel into the box, Emmett showed me how to work the gold pan.

We sat on the edge of the creek together. He dipped water into the pan and swirled it around. "Slowly now, you see?"

I nodded and he gave me the pan. I swirled it around, sloshing the water over the sides.

"No, no." He took the pan out of my hands. "Slowly, slowly. You don't want to dump out the gold."

I tried it again, watching the sand and gravel carefully as it went over the rim with the water.

"That's enough." He took the pan back and sorted through the remaining gravel with his fingers. "No flakes of color in here. Let's try another panful."

We tried pan after pan. The sun was blazing down on us. I couldn't take off my sweat-soaked shirt because of the mosquitoes and gnats buzzing around our heads. It wasn't until after our lunch of hardtack and dried beef that Emmett found yellow flakes in the pan. "Look at that, Bucky! Gold!"

I bent over his pan. Sure enough, he was right. I smiled up at Emmett. His grin was so huge I could see the lump of chewing tobacco tucked in the pocket of his cheek.

Uncle Tanner
Weakens

Every day it was the same thing. Shovel muck into the sluice box, wash it down with water, scrape the gravel from the riffles, and pan the gravel for gold. Emmett kept his half of the gold in a leather pouch he called his poke. Pa and Uncle Tanner's flakes sat in jars above our bunks. As the weeks went by, I watched the first jar slowly fill, and then the second and the third ones.

"How many jars will it take to pay for a hardware store?" I asked Pa one evening when we were sitting on the cabin steps. It was late, but it was still light.

We were so far north that in the middle of summer the sun dipped out of sight around two o'clock in the morning and came back up in an hour.

Pa looked down at me. "You getting homesick for your ma?"

"A little," I admitted.

"Me, too." He hung both his thumbs from his dusty red suspenders and tilted his head. "I think if the pay dirt holds out, we should have enough by September. And if we're real lucky, and if we work real hard, maybe we can go home on a boat."

I jumped off the steps. "Let's get the water going in the sluice box."

I crossed off the days on Emmett's wall calendar. Just before bedtime, as I blackened out the twenty-sixth of July, I looked down at my hands. They were brown and rough, and it seemed to me that they were getting larger. I knew my arms were. I decided to add a drawing of my muscles in my letter to Ma and Nellie.

The next morning at breakfast, Emmett said, "I think we should take our gold to Dawson, have it weighed, and exchange it for Canadian dollars. It ain't a good idea to have too much sitting in the cabin. Too many stampeders have found out all the creeks ain't lined with gold."

Uncle Tanner's face lit up. "I'll go."

Pa said, "Fine. I want to stop at the post office."

I put down my fork. "Can I go?"

"No." Emmett shook his head. "It's a long hike. Two men can do it faster. One of us will stay here with you."

"I'll take your gold, Emmett," Uncle Tanner offered, "and show Clint a bit of the town."

"No thanks, Tanner. I take care of my own gold."

"Well, it's you and me then, Emmett," Pa said. "My letter's ready. Have you got one, Bucky?"

I sprang to my feet, snatched my letter off my bunk, and gave it to Pa.

After Pa and Emmett left, Uncle Tanner sat at the wooden table drinking coffee and pulling on his mustache. Maybe he was disappointed to be left behind. He was slow getting up to start the water flowing in the sluice box.

When he did, he let it pour through too fast and the gravel snapped off the riffles like popcorn. Twice I thought I saw lumps of yellow bounce in the air and down to the pile of tailings at the end of the sluice box.

I kept my mouth shut, though, and went on shoveling from Emmett's winter mounds of dirt. I figured Uncle Tanner'd bite my head off if I dared to suggest he was doing anything wrong.

After lunch, he said he was going fishing. He didn't invite me along.

I hurried down to the tailings. I don't know how

46

many hours went by or how much gravel I sifted through. I know my fingers were raw from scooping up handfuls of tailings and tossing them into the creek after I found no yellow color.

I was about to give up when I spotted a nugget. A real gold nugget. It was a lump about as big as the end

of my little finger, smoothly rounded in places and pitted in others.

I put it in my pants pocket and pawed through the tailings, hoping to find a second one. I never did. Finally, my arms gave in and I trudged up to the cabin for supper.

Uncle Tanner fried fish for us. He didn't say much to me and I didn't tell him about my nugget. I went to bed bubbling inside with my secret. Pa and Emmett came back after I was asleep.

At breakfast, Pa gave me the page of Ma's letter that had my name on it. She wrote that summer didn't seem the same without my wet bathing suit hanging on the back porch railing. She said she missed me and, when I got home, she'd make me another coconut cake and a pitcher of lemonade.

"When do we get to leave?" I asked Pa. "How much money did the gold bring?"

Pa's blue eyes twinkled. "Plenty! If the pay dirt holds out, we should be leaving in a month."

"What?" Uncle Tanner spoke sharply. "I thought you'd stay the winter with me. It's Emmett's turn to go down to the States."

"No," Pa told him. "I want my family together. As soon as I have our savings replaced and the cost of a hardware store, I'll sign my part of the claim back to you."

Uncle Tanner didn't argue, but I could see he was disappointed. I don't think he's the kind of a person who would like to spend a dark winter all by himself. At 50 degrees below zero, I sure wouldn't.

For another month, the four of us worked the sluice box and panned out the gold. The mosquitoes still swarmed and the sun burned, but every time I crossed a day off the calendar, I grew happier.

Near the end of August, Emmett said again, "We'd better get the gold dust to Dawson."

This time, Uncle Tanner jumped up to gather the jars off the shelf. "Let's go," he said to Emmett.

Pa looked startled. I thought he was about to object to Uncle Tanner's carrying our gold, but I guess he didn't know how. After all, Uncle Tanner had had to stay behind the first time.

That day, Pa and I worked the sluice box alone. After supper, I showed him my nugget and asked if I could keep it as a present for Ma. He nodded. "I think you've earned it."

A little later, I crawled up on my bunk. Pa sat at the table, waiting for Emmett and Uncle Tanner's return. I awoke in the middle of the night to hear Pa and Emmett talking.

"He just weakens when he gets around cards," Emmett was saying.

"Bucky!" Pa called out to me. "Get up and pack all your gear."

Trying to figure out what was going on, I slowly climbed out of my bunk.

"Fast!" Pa ordered. He was shoving his clothes into his sack. I did the same with mine.

Emmett shook Pa's hand when we were ready to leave. Before shaking mine, Emmett walked over to my bunk and pulled off the bearskin. "Here. I'll trade you this for your mosquito netting."

"You bet! Thanks. Thanks a lot." I tied the bearskin to my pack with the ribbon from the mosquito netting.

Pa didn't have anything to say after we left the creek and marched hour after hour up the Klondike River. When I took peeks at his face, it looked as hard as stone. I'd never seen him this mad before.

I was worn out by the time we reached Dawson City. It seemed like ten more saloons had been built during the summer. Pa made me stay outside while he went in to check every one.

I sat on the boardwalk waiting for him, wondering if Uncle Tanner had lost all our gold. And wondering how long it would take to fill three more jars. The Yukon River freezes in September and if we weren't out by then, we'd have to stay the winter.

Each time Pa came out of a saloon, his face looked grayer and harder. He marched on down the boardwalk to the next one without a word to me. I thought of Ma and Nellie and the Christmas tree we had every year. And the Thanksgiving turkey.

It was all I could do to keep from crying as Pa swung out the doors of another saloon and stamped across

the street to the Monte Carlo. I followed after him with a sick stomach. It was almost morning. I was sure it was too late to save our gold even if Pa found Uncle Tanner.

I was watching another skinny horse tug a wagon down the street when Pa finally came out of the Monte Carlo. He was pulling his shirt down over his money belt.

Putting an arm around my shoulder, he asked, "How would you like to go to the Fairview Hotel and get a bath before we find a boat for home?"

I stared up into his face. "You got our money?"

"We've got ours. Tanner lost his."

"What'll happen to him?"

"Him? He'll have to spend the winter digging up frozen muck." Then Pa became stern. "But you don't tell your ma about this. She loves her brother."

"Oh, I won't. When do you think we can leave?"

"The bartender told me a paddle-wheeler pulls out of Dawson tomorrow morning. Would you like to be on that?"

"You bet," I said.

There were real beds in the cabins on the riverboat. I spread the bearskin on mine, lay down on the black fur, and tossed my gold nugget in the air. In six weeks I'd be drinking lemonade and eating coconut cake.

My pa smiled down at me. "What are you going to do with that red ribbon you've got tied to the bearskin's tail?"

"Nellie wanted it," I told him. "I'm taking it home to her."

ABOUT THIS BOOK

Bucky, Nellie, Clint, Hope, Uncle Tanner, Emmett, Mr. Martin, and Trixie came from my imagination. The Alaskan gold rush, however, is part of the history of the 1890s. A ship really docked in Seattle in 1897 with a boat full of miners loaded with gold.

Soapy Smith really ruled over the city of Skagway. He came to a bad end, though. In the summer of 1898, he was killed in a shoot-out and could terrorize the stampeders no more.

The stampeders included men, women, and a few children, along with dogs, horses, and even goats and cows. Most of the animals died along the way. So many horses died that one place on the White Pass Trail was named Dead Horse Gulch.

Some people did grow rich in the Yukon, but many, like Uncle Tanner, gambled away their money and died poor.

In 1899, news of another gold strike came from Nome City. Eight thousand miners poured out of Dawson City to head for western Alaska. That brought the Klondike River boom to an end.

When I told my friends and family that I was going to write a story about the gold rush, they generously lent me their books about Alaska. It is close to Washington State, where we live, and most of us have visited there.

The year I was two, my parents moved from Seattle to Ketchikan, Alaska. We didn't stay long enough for me to remember the town. However, my mother brought back Indian baskets, a large bear hide, a pin of gold nuggets, and a book of poems, *The Spell of the Yukon,* written by Robert Service in 1907.

The bear hide was on our floor in the living room throughout my early childhood. I lay upon its rough black fur, slipped my hands into its mouth, and fingered the curved claws.

My grandmother sent my brothers and me a five-dollar gold piece every year for our birthdays. I planned how I would spend my gold piece weeks before it arrived.

When I was fourteen, I adopted Service's books of poems. As I recited the verses to myself I imagined the Yukon winters of long ago, the men possessed by gold, and the howl of the timber wolves. After I grew up, my mother gave me her pin of gold nuggets, and now I have two wolf hybrids of my own.

B.D.